Fairytale Frankie

and the Mermaid Escapade

For Ana and Pepa - G G ★

Rhodes x - S L

For the Magical Mrs Rhodes

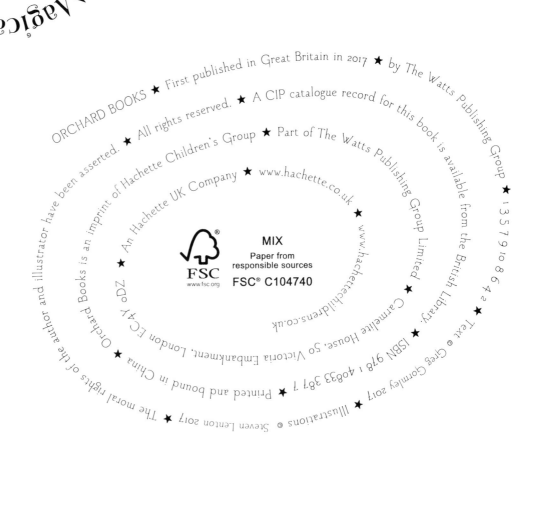

ORCHARD BOOKS ★ First published in Great Britain in 2017 ★ by The Watts Publishing Group

All rights reserved. ★ A CIP catalogue record for this book is available from the British Library.

Orchard Books is an imprint of Hachette Children's Group ★ Part of The Watts Publishing Group Limited

An Hachette UK Company ★ www.hachette.co.uk

www.hachettechildrens.co.uk

Carmelite House, 50 Victoria Embankment, London EC4Y 0DZ

Printed and bound in China

ISBN 978 1 40833 387 7

The moral rights of the author and illustrator have been asserted. ★ Illustrations © Steven Lenton 2017

Text © Greg Gormley 2017

1 3 5 7 9 10 8 6 4 2

MIX
Paper from responsible sources
FSC® C104740
www.fsc.org

Fairytale Frankie

and the Mermaid Escapade

Greg Gormley

Steven Lenton

ORCHARD

Frankie **loved** fairytales.
She **really**, **really** loved them.
So, one sunny afternoon at the
seaside, she was rather surprised
and delighted to find . . .

... a *little* **mermaid** sitting on a rock.

"Hello," said Frankie, "are you coming for a swim?"

"I'm afraid of the **sea monster**," the mermaid said. "The sea monster is **BIG** and I'm only little."

"I'm sure there is no monster," said Frankie, "but let's be big and brave together just in case."

They were playing in the shallows
when a voice boomed out,

"ATTENTION, ATTENTION!
BEWARE OF A MASSIVE
SEA MONSTER IN THE AREA!"

A **wizard lifeguard** appeared in a flash of stars.
"The sea monster **IS** massive," cried the mermaid,
swimming for shore, "and I'm little!"

"Honestly," tutted Frankie, "you're frightening my new friend."

"Sorry," said the wizard. "I'm a bit frightened of the sea monster myself."

"Well, I'm not sure how useful a lifeguard you are," said Frankie, "but maybe the three of us can be big and brave together."

Soon they were happily bobbing up and down on the waves when a **surfing prince** appeared.

"Hey, dudes," he said, "you'd better catch the next wave out of here . . . there is a seriously

HUGE sea monster around."

"The sea monster is HUGE," cried the
mermaid, getting in a flap, "and I'm little!"
"I'm a bit frightened myself," said the wizard.
"I don't dig monsters," agreed the prince.
"There is NO huge monster,"
said Frankie. "And, anyway,
the four of us can be
big and brave together."

Soon they were all having fun watching
the prince doing fancy tricks, until . . .

. . . a beardie pirate sailed into view. "Turn about!" he hollered. "There be a GIGANTIC sea monster in these here waters!"

"Sea monster!"
squawked the pirate's parrot.
"The sea monster is GIGANTIC,"
cried the mermaid, swimming
around and around, "and I'm little!"
"I'm sure the five of us can be big
and brave together," said Frankie,
in a not-so-sure way. "There probably
isn't a monster anyway."

But, just at that moment, the sea started to **Stir**.

It **bubbled** and **churned**... it **swirled** and **whirled**...

"A beast from the deep!"
said the beardie pirate, and **dived** hat-first into his treasure chest.

"A dreadful sea-dude!" said the surfer prince. He **flipped** his board over and pretended to be a fish.

"A fearsome thing!" said the wizard. He turned himself into a crab and hid in his hat.

"That's not **AT ALL** helpful," muttered
Frankie. "It's up to me to be big and brave."
She swam in front of her friend.
"I'll protect you!" she said . . .

. . . but it was too late.

Something was emerging from the deep . . .

slowly, scarily . . .

... the monster appeared!

"Oh look, he's adorable!" laughed Frankie.
"That must be the **smallest** sea monster
in the deep blue sea," said the mermaid.
"Hi there," the monster said, in
a sweet and salty voice.

"You are not **big** or **massive** or **huge** or **gigantic!**" said the mermaid to the monster. "You're little, like me."

"And you're small, like me," said the sea monster. "But we can still have **BIG** fun!" smiled Frankie.

So they did –
BIG, MASSIVE, HUGE, GIGA